BLIND DATES FOR LONELY GORGONS

AN OBSCURE ACADEMY STORY

LAURA GREENWOOD

 Created with Vellum

BLURB

As a gorgon, Thalia has always avoided dating so she doesn't risk turning someone into stone, but when her best friend convinces her to sign up for the Valentine's Blind Date event, everything changes.

When Thalia meets Evander, there's an instant connection, even if he doesn't ask conventional first date questions. But will he still feel the same when he discovers the truth about what she is?

-

Blind Dates For Lonely Gorgons is a light-hearted gorgon academy m/f romance set at Obscure Academy. It is Thalia and Evander's complete story.

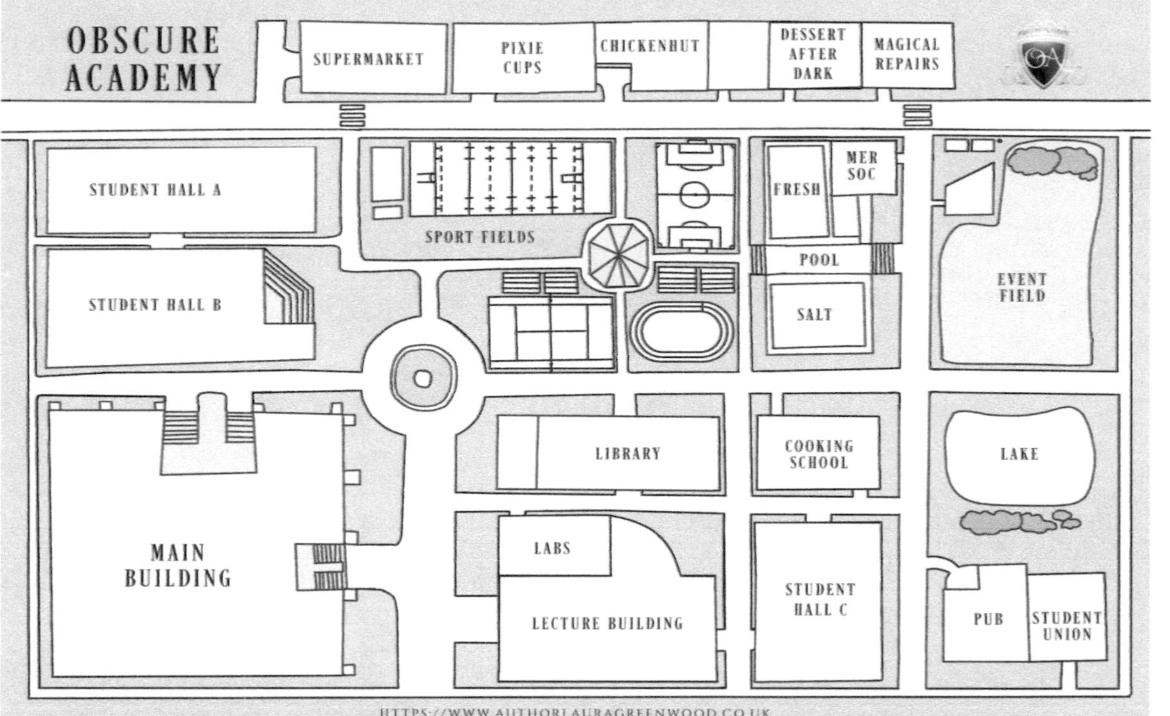

OBSCURE ACADEMY
SUPERMARKET
PIXIE CUPS
CHICKENHUT
DESSERT AFTER DARK
MAGICAL REPAIRS
STUDENT HALL A
STUDENT HALL B
SPORT FIELDS
FRESH
MER SOC
POOL
SALT
EVENT FIELD
LAKE
MAIN BUILDING
LIBRARY
LABS
LECTURE BUILDING
COOKING SCHOOL
STUDENT HALL C
PUB
STUDENT UNION
HTTPS://WWW.AUTHORLAURAGREENWOOD.CO.UK

ONE

THALIA

MY GLASSES SLIP down my nose where I'm looking down at the two mugs of tea I'm carrying. I wrinkle my nose to try and make them go back into place. If I enter the room with them not covering my eyes properly, then my best friend would be in big trouble.

I put my back to my bedroom door and push through. "Close your eyes," I call out, trusting that she'll follow instructions.

I turn slowly and squint my eyes just in case. I'll take any precautions I can take to minimise the risk of turning Michaela into stone. And I've been managing that since I was old enough to understand what I am and how my gorgon powers work.

Satisfied her eyes are closed, I set the mugs down on my desk and push my glasses up my nose so they're sat more snuggly against my face. So long as she doesn't look me directly in the eyes while I'm not wearing them, my magic won't work on her. I'm not precisely sure how the glasses work. They've been part of me for as long as I can remember. My parents probably explained how it all worked at some point, but I can't remember it.

"Is it safe to open them again?" Michaela asks.

"Mmhmm."

She opens her eyes and smiles at me. "Glasses fall down?"

I nod. She gets it. She wears them herself, though just for bad vision rather than anything magical. Sometimes I envy her, but then I remember she has her own magical problems to deal with.

"Sometimes I wonder what it would be like to live without them," she says, touching her dark round frames. "But it's such a strange concept that I'm not sure I'd be able to last more than a day."

"I would. I've dreamt about it my whole life." I sigh wistfully. "But it's never going to change."

"You don't know that. There are witches and

warlocks coming up with new treatments for magical maladies every day," Michaela counters.

"But my problem isn't a magical malady, it's just my inborn magic."

"They have people working on something to help vampires come out during the day, I'm sure they're trying to find a way for gorgons to stop turning people into stone."

"True, but there are a lot more vampires than there are gorgons."

"I don't think that's any reason for them not to be researching things. If they can help one person, then it's a good thing."

I repress a sigh. There's no use pointing out to her that most people aren't as fundamentally good as she is. Just because she thinks it's a worthy cause to help people like me, it doesn't mean that other people do. Far from it. My people have been struggling for years, and we're lucky not to still be in hiding like some of the other dangerous supernaturals.

I pick up my cup of tea and blow across the top of it. It's still too hot to drink, but I want something to do with my hands to break the slight tension in the air. I love Michaela, but sometimes she's too naive for the world.

"Have you seen the event the student union is

putting on for Valentine's Day?" Michaela asks as she reaches out for the other mug.

She seems to have realised the topic of conversation needs changing, but somehow I don't get the impression this is going to be any better.

"I haven't," I respond warily. I avoid everything that has the words *Valentine's Day* in the title of it. Not because I have anything against it, but because it makes me feel more lonely than ever.

Being a gorgon isn't very fun. Particularly when it comes to trying to have a love life. People tend to be put off by the idea of a steamy makeout session ending up with them turned into stone.

"It's a blind date thing. Everyone fills out a questionnaire and then they match people up. It sounds kind of fun," she says.

"For you," I mutter.

Michaela sighs and looks over her mug at me. "There must be something you can do. You can look at me without turning me into stone," she points out.

"I know, but that's different."

"So you keep saying, but I don't understand *how* it's different."

I sigh. I've never tried talking to anyone about this, but maybe that should change. Michaela and I have spent a lot of time together and she's never made me feel badly about what I am. I can trust her with this.

"It's just that the idea of dating someone is that you end up close to them," I mumble.

"It is, yes. Or I suppose it is if you want to get close to someone. There are people who don't care for romantic partners at all..."

"That's off-topic."

"I suppose it is." She smiles reassuringly at me. "Go on."

"It's just that if I was *close* to someone..."

"You mean in bed."

"I don't just mean that," I admit. "But partly that, yes. if I'm in bed with someone, then there are more chances for my glasses to fall off, and if that happens, I might turn them into stone."

"Ah, and that's not the kind of rock hard you want in the bedroom," she quips.

I don't do anything to suppress my groan. "You know how tired that joke is for gorgons, right?"

She chuckles, clearly amused by herself even if she shouldn't be. "I'm sorry, it was just right there and I knew I had to say it."

I sigh. "The joke is crass, but it's true. *Sorry I turned you into stone last night, honey,* gets old really fast."

"It does if you call your boyfriends honey."

"Mickie," I scold.

"All right, sorry. I'll try and stop. You know I just can't help it."

A small doting smile crosses my face. I know she's not doing it to be cruel. "But you get what I mean."

"I see how it could be a problem, yes. But I think I might have a solution."

I frown. "What kind of solution?"

"I don't want to say yet."

I narrow my eyes at her, worrying about what she might have planned. Michaela isn't known for having the best plans.

"Don't look at me like that." She holds her hands up as if I have no reason to be worried about what she's going to do. "I promise I have nothing but good intentions."

"It's not your intentions I'm worried about," I mutter.

"I'd be annoyed at you, but you have a point," she concedes. "I promise that this time I'm not going to let anything bad happen. I'm going to find a way for you to go on a date and not have to worry about the end of the night."

"It's not the end of the first night I'm worried about."

"I know. But if it works once, then hopefully it'll

work every time. And don't rule it out on date one. You never know what might happen. Maybe he'll be super hot but you don't want to go on a second date."

"Then why would I want to sleep with him?"

"For fun." She cocks her head to the side and studies me intently.

"Ah." I don't know what to tell her. I've only ever had one boyfriend and it was a bit of a disaster when it came to that part of things. Fumbling around in the dark so we didn't risk me turning him into stone wasn't particularly fun.

"But it doesn't matter whether or not you do, just that you have the choice to," she points out.

"True."

"And I'm going to make it happen."

A loud sigh escapes me. "Fine, I'll sign up to the blind date event."

"Excellent." The satisfied smile on her face reveals just how important she thinks this is, though I'm not sure why.

But I suppose it might be fun, especially if she can find a way to actually help me.

TWO

Thalia

Why have I signed up to go blind dating? This is foolish. It goes against everything I've ever been taught about being a gorgon.

I need to calm down. I had to fight to get my parents to let me come to Obscure Academy, they wanted me to stay home where it's safer, but I wanted a more normal academy experience. That means taking part in things like this. If I don't take this chance, then it's a waste.

"I'm sorry, I'm sorry, I meant to be here twenty minutes ago," Michaela says as she pushes through my open door and sits on my bed. "I just had to deal with a last-minute thing."

"Would that last-minute thing have a name?" I ask.

She chuckles. "It has the name potion." She pulls out a small bottle and places it on my desk.

I eye it warily. "Did you make that?" I ask.

She sighs. "Why does everyone always ask that?"

"Previous experience."

"I'd be mad about that, but you have a point."

"So, did you?"

"Kind of. I had help."

"What kind of help?"

She sighs. "I knew this was important, so I asked the best potion brewer on campus for help. Between us we figured out everything we needed to."

I'm still not convinced, but even if Michaela's potion-making skills aren't the best, I do trust her.

"What do I owe you for it?" I ask.

"Nothing."

"But this potion brewer must have wanted something in return for their help."

Michaela blushes furiously. "You can't help with what he wants."

"Mickie!" I can't believe she'd do something like that for me.

"Not that," she dismisses. "It's just a date. And I want to go on it, so it's not even a bad thing."

"Ah, so your errand did have a name."

"It's Owen."

"In which case, I can't wait to meet him," I say. "And thank him for the potion. But what does it do?"

"It should mean that you don't have to wear your glasses and you won't turn your date into stone."

My mouth falls open as disbelief swirls through me. "Are you serious?"

She nods. "So I asked around and someone else had heard of it too."

"Why does she even have a recipe like that?"

"I asked, but she said something about having a lot of fun in her youth and I didn't want to pry any further."

I chuckle, understanding exactly what she means. My own grandmother can get a bit vocal about some of her younger antics. "I don't blame you."

"Anyway, it doesn't matter why she had it, or why it exists. It does, and that's it." She points to the bottle. "It should last for forty-eight hours, so as long as you organise your date for tomorrow, it'll still be working."

"Is it really safe?"

"There's only one way to find out," Michaela says.

"What do you mean?"

She cocks her head to the side and gives me a funny look. "You can drink the potion, take your glasses off, and look me in the eye. I didn't think that bit was confusing."

"I can't do that. What if I turn you into stone?"

She shrugs. "It's not permanent, right?"

"It shouldn't be, no. But I don't know how long you'd be stuck like that, and I have no idea if there'll be any lasting damage." Worry worms its way through me. I don't want to turn my best friend into stone, especially when she's one of the only people who spends time with me regularly.

"It's a risk I'm willing to take," she assures me. "And if you turn me into stone, then it'll be an interesting story to tell people later."

"You're weird."

She laughs lightly. "If you're only just figuring that out, then I worry for you."

"Won't your flatmates miss you if you end up spending the next couple of days in my room?"

She shrugs. "Maybe, but you know what my flat's like, there's always people coming and going. Plus we have the invisible guy in room eight."

"You still haven't seen him?"

"No one has. We're only sure he's there because Fiona and Jeremy can hear him through the walls."

"So strange," I murmur.

"Very. But you're stalling. Drink the potion, Thalia. I'm not going to be mad at you if it doesn't work, we'll still be friends."

I sigh. "Fine. But if this goes wrong, I'm holding you fully accountable."

"Good."

I reach out for the potion and pass it from one hand to the other. Slowly, I pull off the cork, but I don't drink it yet. A small part of me is hesitating. This isn't something I've ever heard of before.

But it's not like I'm picking it up from a shelf and trying it for the first time. Michaela brought it to me, and while she's not good at making potions, she comes from a line of powerful witches.

I take a deep breath and swallow down the potion. It tastes earthy, but not unpleasant. I wait for some kind of tingling sensation to overcome me, but it doesn't.

"Is that it?" I ask. "Is it supposed to do anything?"

"I've no idea, I've never known anyone who took it before."

"And there's really only one way to find out if it's worked?"

She shrugs. "I assume so. Take the glasses off."

I touch them gently, unsure if I'm ready to do this. But I need to test this before the date tonight.

My eyes flutter closed as if by reflex as I pull my glasses off.

"It's not going to work if you're not looking at me," Michaela says, amusement dancing in her tone.

"I know. I'm just nervous," I admit. "The only people I've ever looked at without my glasses on are other gorgons."

"And that's not a problem?" she asks.

I shake my head. "We can't turn each other into stone."

"At least that's something. Now look at me."

I lift my head and slowly open my eyes, preparing myself for the guilt that'll take over when she freezes.

My gaze meets hers and I wait for the inevitable to happen.

Only it doesn't.

A wide smile spreads over her face. "It worked?"

"I mean, I think so. But maybe we should wait a few hours before I go in front of other people without my glasses."

She nods. "Understandable."

I put my glasses back on straight away.

"There's still more than twelve hours until the date event," she says. "So that gives us plenty of time to make sure I'm un-stoney."

"Thank you." Emotions choke my words, but I

manage to get them out. "You have no idea what this means to me."

"You'd do the same for me if you could," she responds. "You're my best friend, and I want to help in whatever way I can."

I nod, unable to say anything. But she knows how grateful I am, and that one day, I'll make it up to her. And not because I feel like I owe her, but because I want to.

She's the kind of friend I've always dreamed of, and I'm lucky to have met her.

THREE

Thalia

I approach the student union bar with nerves fluttering in my stomach.

"You're going to be fine," Michaela promises.

"I didn't even say anything," I point out.

"You didn't have to, I know you well enough to be able to tell what your serious face means."

A small smile creeps onto my face. "What if the potion doesn't work?"

"You don't have to worry about that too much right now," she points out. "And you can wear your glasses if you want."

I touch the skin by my eyes, still unused to the

way to the way it feels not to be wearing glasses. Even when I'm alone in my room I keep them on. Not because I'm at risk of turning anyone into stone there, but because I'm so used to wearing them that I don't think about taking them off until it's time to sleep.

I pat my pocket to make sure I still have them and sigh with relief when I find them still there.

"I'm going to try and go without them," I say. "You've gone to a lot of trouble for this potion for me, I don't want to waste that."

"I appreciate that, but if you're not comfortable, then you shouldn't do it."

"And here you are trying to push me outside my comfort zone in doing this." I gesture towards the building in front of us, knowing I'm going to have to go inside sooner rather than later. The blind date event starts in about ten minutes and I've already paid for my entry ticket.

"I'm sorry, I shouldn't have done that. We can turn around and go for a drink at the pub instead, if you want."

I shake my head. "We're here now. And you're right about this being good for me." I'm certainly not making the most of my time at Obscure Academy by sitting at home and hanging out with the same person all the time. "All right, let's get inside."

Before she can respond, I push through the door and into the student union. Even from this distance, I can hear the people in the bar downstairs, which is only making my nerves worse.

But I've come too far to back out now.

I make my way down the flight of stairs that leads to the bar. The last time I was here was during Freshers week when it was packed with other first-year students all celebrating the end of our first week as students. The place looks so different now, mostly because of how many fewer people there are.

The whole bar is decorated with hearts and pink tablecloths. It's kind of over the top, but at the same time, it fits with the theme of the event.

"Hi," a cheery woman with a name tag announcing her name is Denise says. "Are you here for the blind date event?"

I nod. "I'm Thalia Montgomery."

She looks down at her clipboard and searches the names. "Ah, yes, here you are. You've been matched with Evander at table seven. Have a good date." She turns away, clearly dismissing me.

Michaela and I head over to the bar to order ourselves some drinks.

"I'll be right here," Michaela promises, gesturing to her spot by the bar. "But I don't think you'll need me, he's cute." She nods towards a table with a number seven written on a small chalkboard at the centre.

She's not wrong, even from this distance, I can tell she's right.

"I'm going to need more than cute if this is going to work," I point out. I nod my thanks to the bartender as he slides our drinks across the bar to us.

"True. But you have ten minutes to make a connection with him and then you have to move on to your next set up."

"I thought this was blind dating, not speed dating." I'm not sure how I'm going to feel about going from one person to the other.

"Maybe it's a mix of both? At least you're not on a stage with people watching you."

A shiver runs down my spine at the thought. She's not wrong about that. I don't think I'd have been able to go through with it if that's the case.

Feedback from a microphone pulls my attention towards where Denise is standing on a stage. "If you'd all take your seats, the first round of dates is about to begin," she announces.

"Good luck," Michaela says.

"Thanks." I think I'm going to need it. I pick up my still full wine glass.

With a deep breath, I make my way over to table

number seven, almost wishing I'd been there before Evander, but I suppose it doesn't matter.

I slide into the seat opposite. "Hi," I say awkwardly.

"Hello," he responds. "I'm Evander."

"Thalia."

"It's nice to meet you." He feels slightly nervous, though I can't figure out what's making me think that.

"Likewise."

I fiddle with the hem of my dress under the table, trying to think of the right kind of questions to ask.

"I've never done this before," I admit. The last thing I want is to make him think my nervousness is any reflection on him when it's really all about me.

"Me neither," he responds. "I'm not sure what even made me sign up."

"For me, it was my best friend. She thinks I don't date enough."

"Do you agree?"

I chuckle dryly. "I'm here, I think that says I agree with her."

"I'm not even sure what question to ask now," he admits.

"I think we're supposed to do classic get to know you questions," I respond. "Things like what's your favourite colour, how many siblings you have, what you're studying, that kind of thing."

"They're very boring questions if you think about it. What good is it for you to know that my favourite colour is yellow, I'm an only child, and that I'm studying to be a chemist."

"It might tell me that you're an evil genius in the making, but that you'll smile happily while you do it." I take a sip of wine, but put my glass down quickly so he doesn't think I'm doing it because I don't want to have a conversation with him.

Evander lets out a small laugh. "That's fair."

"So what questions do you propose instead?"

"I think we need to skip straight to the real questions."

"Such as..." I'm intrigued to find out what he might have in store.

"Would you rather be a pirate or a ninja?" he asks.

I let out a small laugh. "That's your real question?"

"Of course. It'll tell me all I need to know about you. So, which would you want to be?"

"Can't I be a pirate ninja?"

"No."

"Hmm, then that's hard. On the one hand, ninja skills would be great, but I don't think I have the grace for it. But I also don't think I have the ruthlessness of a pirate. Though maybe I could be a revenge pirate," I muse.

"What's a revenge pirate?"

"The kind that goes around protecting people who can't protect themselves instead of just pillaging and looting. I'd get to keep the spoils anyway, fulfilling my role as a pirate, but I won't have to go around attacking innocent people." I reach up and tuck a strand of hair behind my ear, as grateful as ever that I don't have snakes for hair like the old legends say gorgons do. I don't even have any partiality to snakes, though I'm sure there are some gorgons who do.

"That's an interesting answer," he admits. "And not what I expected."

"What can I say? I like to surprise people." I flash him a smile, finally feeling as if I'm managing to relax into the conversation. "So now it's my turn to ask a question, right?"

"Mmhmm. And it can't be the same one."

"You're just making that rule up."

"Maybe, but it's our date, we can make up all the rules we want," Evander says.

"Except about when it will end." I glance at the clock, surprised to find we don't have much time left at all. "Okay, so if you could only eat one kind of food for the rest of your life, what would it be?" It feels like a silly question to ask someone I've just met, but I guess that's part of what we're supposed to be doing.

"Breakfast food," he responds with a certainty that makes it clear he's thought about this before.

"Okay, but why?"

"Because it can vary so much. If I want steak for breakfast tomorrow, I can do that. But if I want waffles with blueberries and maple syrup the next day, I can do that too."

"That's almost as much of a cheat as saying salad."

"Because everything can be a salad?"

"Exactly."

"I do like finding loopholes in questions," he admits with an impish grin.

"Yet you wouldn't allow me to choose a pirate ninja."

"That's because you asked whether you could."

"Sneaky." But secretly, I like it. He managed to get us talking by using it, and I think that goes a long way towards forgiveness.

A gong sounds, drawing confusion from me until I realise that means it's the end of the dates.

"Attention blind daters," Denise calls out with her microphone. "I'll be coming around and giving you all your next table number momentarily. After you've received it, you should make your way to your next date."

"Why does it always feel like bad timing when announcements like that happen?" Evander asks.

"I know. We were just getting into the weird questions," I agree, surprised to find myself feeling somewhat regretful that I'm going to have to leave his company.

"Would it be too forward of me to ask you for your number already?" he blurts out.

For a moment, I consider saying it would be, but I stop before I do, realising that I want him to have it.

I grab a napkin and one of the pens from the middle of the table and scribble it on, pushing it over to him. "I look forward to getting your next weird question."

"Dating etiquette says I need to wait three days."

"Dating etiquette doesn't seem to have caught up with the idea of instant communication," I counter. "I won't mind if you don't wait that long." And if we chose one another for our date at the end of the night, I believe we're technically supposed to go out on another date tomorrow, though I'm not sure how they're going to enforce something like that.

"Then you'll hear from me soon," he promises.

Denise approaches our table with her hostess

smile firmly in place. "Thalia you're going to Brad at table three, and Evander, you're going to Daisy at table six."

"Thanks," I say, trying to smile as enthusiastically at her as she is at me, but fearing I'm not managing.

She disappears before either of us can say anything to her.

"I guess this is goodbye for now," I say to Evander.

He nods. "But hopefully not for long."

I hope not either. "Good luck on your next date," I say.

"You too."

I grab my still almost full glass of wine and head over to the empty table three. Just as I take a seat, my phone buzzes in my pocket. With Brad nowhere to be seen yet, I pull it out and check it, surprised to find an unknown number on the screen.

< It was really nice to meet you. E. >

I chuckle, realising who it must be from.

< Three minutes instead of three days is breaking the dating rules a lot. > I hit send before I can overthink it.

< I've never been good at following rules. >

< It made for an interesting date. I liked it. >

< Me too. I hope your next date is as original as me. >

I let out a small laugh, surprised by how much I seem to have actually connected with someone already

"Hey," a male voice says.

I look up to find a tall guy with sandy hair standing in front of the table.

"Are you Thalia?"

I nod. "I'm guessing you're Brad?"

"Yes." He slides into the seat opposite me. "So, how many siblings do you have?"

I paste on the best smile I can muster and settle in to answer the basic questions Evander had somehow known to avoid. He's right. They are boring, I just hadn't realised how dull they were until it was pointed out to me. Somehow, I feel as if my whole perspective on dating is going to be changed by tonight.

And it's probably only going to make things harder.

FOUR

THALIA

"WHAT DO you think of this one?" I ask Michaela, holding up a dress for her to inspect.

She scrunches up her face and cocks her head to the side. "No."

"I like this dress."

"So do I, but it's for a day at the beach, not for a first date," she says.

"Wasn't last night our first date?" I ask.

"No, that was just your meeting. You have to have the meet-cute first, and then you go on the date. After that there are a few ways it can go."

"You've been watching too many rom-coms," I

mutter, putting the dress back in my wardrobe and searching for the next one to check with her.

I select a pretty black dress with a rose pattern.

She shakes her head. "Sit down, let me pick you out something."

"If you insist." I sit down on my bed and reach for my phone.

No texts, which wasn't a surprise. Evander said in his message earlier that he had back-to-back classes this afternoon. I'm lucky that I don't, it gives me time to work out what I'm going to wear on our date.

Michaela hums as she searches through my clothes for the perfect outfit. "I'm still surprised that you said yes to this."

"You told me I had to."

"Only if you found someone you liked."

"Exactly."

She pulls out a black dress with a flared knee-length skirt and a low neckline covered in sheer material. "This one."

"Is it not a bit..." I wave my hand around my chest area.

"It's your dress."

"I've never worn it," I admit. "I've been trying to pluck up the courage to on a night out, but every time, I chicken out."

"Put it on and we'll see how it looks," she instructs.

I sigh and take it from her. I slip into my bathroom, but don't close the door.

"So, how did Evander convince you to go on a date with him?" she asks.

"He messaged me during my second date last night," I admit. "And then we were chatting for a few hours after. He asked me if I wanted to meet him for a drink, and I said yes before I thought twice about it."

Her shocked silence says it all.

I slip out of my comfortable clothes, and slip on the dress. "Are you sure the potion is going to work for tonight too?"

I step out of the bathroom so she can see how it looks.

"Oh yes, that's the one," she says about the dress. "But you can't wear that bra."

"I wasn't planning on it." If I'm going on a date, then I'm going to wear nice underwear, even if I don't plan on anyone seeing it. There's always something confidence-boosting about wearing a matching set.

"Okay. Good. And yes, you should be all set. Owen said that he did some tests on it after we finished the batch and he's certain that it'll work."

"Okay." I'm still not completely convinced, but so long as I take my glasses with me, I think it'll be all right. I smooth down my dress and try not to focus too much on the nerves building inside me. "What if this goes badly? Maybe I should call it off."

I flop down onto the bed and rest my face in my hands.

Michaela sighs and scoots closer to me so she can put an arm around my shoulders. "Do you really think it's going to go badly?"

"Maybe when I tell him I'm a gorgon, you know what people get like when they discover that. They just end up running away."

"I didn't," Michaela points out.

"You're not trying to date me."

"So? You said everyone went running when they found out, but I prove that's not true. Maybe you should give Evander more credit. And if you're not sure that you want to tell him yet, then you don't have to. You only have to tell him if you're going to have kids or something."

"Won't he find it suspicious if I don't tell him?" There's a whininess in my voice that I don't like, but I can't avoid the way I'm feeling.

"Has he told you what he is?"

"No."

"Then you have nothing to worry about. Or

maybe you should be worried about what he is instead. There must be a reason he's keeping it quiet too. But maybe he'll tell you that he's something even more dramatic than a gorgon, and then what you are is almost a relief."

Despite my worries, I let out a small laugh. "What could be worse than a gorgon?"

"I'm not sure. Maybe something that sets things on fire a lot? I've heard salamanders can be easy to anger and quick to burn down the house."

I shake my head in bemusement. "I suppose you have a point. But maybe that's not such a problem if I can turn the salamander into stone before it does something like that."

"See, you're already looking at this in a different way." She pats me on the arm. "Besides, I'm bringing Owen with me to the pub too, so if you need to get out of there, all you have to do is give me a signal and then I'll come to your rescue."

"You're bringing Owen?" I try to keep the surprise out of my voice, but it comes through anyway.

"Mmhmm. Is that a problem?"

"Of course not. I just didn't realise you'd be going on your first date so soon."

A blush rises to her cheeks. "I didn't want to make him wait."

"Is there a chance you actually like him?" I ask.

"He's nice," she admits. "And I want to know if it's going to go anywhere sooner rather than later or I'm going to start overthinking things. You're not the only one who has trouble trusting people won't judge you for something you can't change about yourself."

"You mean your lack of potions skills?"

She grimaces. "That's the one. How many witches have you heard of who can't even make a basic potion? My flatmates even do everything they can to avoid me making them cups of tea."

"That's because your tea is awful," I admit.

She sighs dramatically. "Maybe it's water I'm no good at," she mutters.

"I'm sorry."

"It's fine. I'm used to it. At least I can do spells." She pulls out her wand and waves it around until a small shower of sparks falls from it.

"See? It isn't all that bad. Sure, the potion thing sucks, but you can do other magic."

"I know. And people here don't care too much about it either. It's actually nice to not have to be perfect all the time." A sadness enters her voice that I don't think I've heard before. She hasn't told me much about how hard it's been to not be good at magic like the rest of her family.

I smile at her, a sense of belonging while I sit here with my first friend who isn't also a gorgon. I never thought I'd have someone like Michaela in my life, but I'm so glad I do.

At least when she pushes me out of my comfort zone, she goes with me to make sure I'm safe.

FIVE

EVANDER

EXCITEMENT FILLS me as I approach the redhead at the bar. The last thing I expected when I went to the blind dating event organised by the academy's cupids was to find someone I actually want to spend time with, but something clicked inside me when I started talking to Thalia, and I was sad when our date ended.

It's a good job we get to have another one.

"Hey," I say with what I hope is a friendly smile. "What would you like?" I gesture towards the bar.

"Just an orange juice, if that's okay?"

I nod, not at all surprised by her request. It makes

sense that she doesn't want to drink on a first-ish date.. I flag down the bartender and order two orange juices.

"You can order something stronger if you want," she says.

"I don't mind. Sometimes it's nice to have some time off from the drinking. I don't know what your flat is like, but mine likes to have some crazy night outs." And there's the fact that I'm taking a potion I don't have any experience with. I trust Owen's potion-making skills, but it's better to be safe than sorry when it comes to mixing it with alcohol.

"Same," she admits. "Though I don't always go with them. Sometimes I prefer to have a quiet night in." She touches her face in a way that makes me wonder if she normally wears glasses.

I push the thought to the side. It's irrelevant whether she does or not, I only notice because I'm overly aware of not having my own on.

I pay for the drinks and hand her one of them. "There's a free booth over there, do you want to go sit there, or would you prefer to stay by the bar?"

"The booth sounds good." She smiles reassuringly at me, convincing me that she's making decisions that she wants to, not that she thinks she has to.

I slide into the booth first so that she's the one

who decides how closely we sit together. The last thing I want to do is make her feel uncomfortable.

She sits next to me and sets her orange juice on the table before shrugging off her coat. She folds it over her arm and glances around, clearly looking for somewhere to put it.

"I can pop it over here?" I suggest, gesturing to the empty chair on the other side of the table.

"Thanks." she hands it to me. "I thought of another question I could ask you."

"Oh?" A small smile lifts at my lips at the thought of her considering what unusual date questions she can ask.

"If you could be any animal, what would you be? And if you're a shifter, you're not allowed to say your real animal." The way she says the last part leaves no doubt in my mind that she expects me to behave.

I let out a small laugh. "I'm not a shifter. That won't be a problem."

"So, what would you be?"

"That's a hard one. I've always felt an affinity to aardvarks."

Surprise flits over her face. "That's so specific."

"You asked the question," I point out.

"I guess I expected you to say something obvious like a lion or a bear."

I raise an eyebrow. "Is that how you see me?"

"I don't know you well enough to be sure about what animal fits you best," she points out. "Unless you're trying to tell me that you already know what animal you think would suit me."

I take a sip of my drink and lean back in my seat while I study her. "A deer."

She cocks her head to the side, as if surprised by my choice. Maybe she's the shifter and I haven't picked her animal. Maybe this isn't a good game to play after all.

"I'm sorry," I say softly. "I didn't mean to insult you."

"What, no, you didn't. I'm sorry, I just got caught up in my thoughts. Why do you think I'm a deer?" she asks.

"I'm not sure," I admit. For a moment, I'm not sure if it's safe to answer, but I push the worry aside. I'm just being me. If she doesn't like it, then that's her problem and we just won't go on another date. "I think it's because you have a sense of curiosity about you, but also gentleness."

"Oh." She tucks a strand of loose hair behind her ear. "I've never thought about it like that."

"So you agree?"

"I'm not sure. I like cats, but that could just be because we have one at home. I've never really thought about what animal I'm the most like," she says.

"That makes sense." I nod along.

"I think it's your turn for the question." She takes a drink.

"I made a list." I reach for my pocket and pull out the piece of paper I've been scribbling thoughts on for the past few days.

"Did you worry we wouldn't have anything to talk about?" she teases.

"Not at all. But I kept thinking of fun things and I wrote them down so I didn't forget them. We don't have to if you don't want."

"No, I like the questions."

I'm glad. I feel like they give us a proper chance to get to know one another and the things that really matter, even if some of the questions are nonsensical. "Okay then, if you had to be mer, what kind of fish would you want your tail to be?"

Laughter bursts from her. "That's a risky question. What if I was mer?"

"I figured you weren't. MerSoc has an extra meeting tonight for some kind of festival, and most of the mer at the academy will be at the swimming pool doing their thing."

"I've always wondered how they manage to live so far away from the sea."

"I suppose it's only a couple of hours by train.

The advantage of living in a small country, I guess. But I've been told by the swim team that the mer take over the salt-water pool for a bit and just sit around and do the normal things we all do at society meetings." It must be quite a sight.

"So they play drinking games and make fun of each other," she says.

"Something like that, but I've never been."

"Meaning you aren't mer," she observes astutely.

"No, I'm not."

"So you're not a shifter, and you're not a mer. And considering the sun was only just setting when we arrived, you're not a vampire either," she muses.

"No, I'm none of those," I agree. "I can tell you if you particularly need to know." The words are out before I think twice about them. At this point, I'm not sure if I want her to ask so I can tell her I'm a gorgon and get it over with, or if I'd prefer to wait a little longer.

To my surprise, she shakes her head and reaches as if to push glasses up her nose. Interesting. She definitely normally wears them. I wish she'd felt comfortable enough to come in them tonight, I think they'd look good on her.

"You don't have to, especially if you're not ready to," she says, taking me by surprise. Somehow I almost managed to forget what we're talking about.

"Then let's leave that conversation for another day," I suggest, trying my best to hide my relief. "You haven't answered the question, though. What kind of fishtail would you want as a mer?"

"It'd be nice to have something graceful, but in reality, I'd probably have a pufferfish tail and end up exploding every time I got embarrassed."

A warm laugh builds within me and bursts free. "That's not the answer I expected."

"You thought I'd say something prettier?"

"Maybe something less honest," I admit.

"That would defeat the point of the game. The whole point is that we actually get to know one another, right?"

"Yes," I confirm.

"Then honest is the only way to go. So, what would your tail be if you were mer?"

"Hmm, give me a second to think about it." I tap my finger against my chin as I consider my options.

Thalia raises an eyebrow. "You didn't do that when you thought about the questions?"

"I did, but now I'm worrying that I didn't give it enough attention."

She shakes her head in bemusement. "Why don't I get us some more drinks while you think about it?" She gestures to my empty glass. "Same again, or do you want something different?"

"I wouldn't mind a cola, please."

"Coming right up." She grabs her bag and heads to the bar, only to be joined seconds later by a dark-haired girl I think I vaguely recognise from the blind dating event. That must be a friend she's arranged to come and keep an eye on things.

That's smart. Safety is important.

They exchange a few words while she flags down the bartender. At least I don't have to worry about her disappearing. This date seems to be going as well as I think it is.

Thalia glances over in my direction and I wave to her.

She smiles back, but turns away when the bartender returns to take the payment from her.

Within a few minutes, Thalia is setting our drinks on the table.

"Is everything all right?" I ask.

She nods. "My friend was just telling me she's heading to a new destination with her date, nothing to worry about," she assures me.

"Are you okay without a chaperone?"

"You're not annoyed I had one to begin with?" she asks.

"No, it's sensible to protect yourself," I point out.

A reassured smile crosses her face. "Well now

we're alone," she says. "So you can tell me what type of tail you'd want to have."

"Hmm. I was going to say a hammerhead shark," I admit.

"Interesting choice. Have you changed your mind?"

"I think it would be a sawfish."

"A sawfish?" she echoes.

"Yes. They look impressive, but they're unwieldy and kind of useless."

She lets out a tinkling laugh that makes me want to hear it many more times before the end of our date. "Is that how you see yourself?"

"Not necessarily, but sometimes these things just fit."

"Hmm true."

The conversation turns to the next question, leaving a growing satisfaction within me that I've found someone who thinks in a similar way to how I do. I could get used to more dates like this, and I hope I get a chance to.

SIX

THALIA

"So, TELL ME ABOUT LAST NIGHT?" Michaela asks as she blows across the top of her travel mug.

I eye the one she brought me warily, wondering why she's brought it when she knows she's terrible at making tea. Especially when I have a perfectly good kettle here.

"I stopped at Pixie Cups on the way," she assures me. "Yours is green tea, not too strong and I haven't touched it other than to bring it to you."

"Thanks." I pick it up and am greeted by the familiar scent of tea. I pop off the lid and a small puff of steam escapes, fogging up my glasses. It smells right, but Michaela's inability to brew potions is more supernatural than we are. It wouldn't surprise me if she could turn it bad even without brewing it herself.

"Now, tell me about the date. Did you have a good time?"

"I did. Thank you for pushing me to do the Blind Date event. I'd never have gone if you hadn't."

"That's something I'm well aware of."

"How did your date go anyway? Was the food good?"

"It was, Owen took me to a late-night café around the corner from the academy. It was really nice," she says.

"Are you going to see him again?"

"Yes. Is that bad? We met because I wanted to brew the potion for you. I don't know if it's weird that we're going to go out on more dates."

A frown pulls at my forehead. "Why would it be bad? I don't think it really matters how you meet, it's what happens after that which matters."

"What if I met him at his wedding to someone named Frances?" she returns quickly. "Does it not matter then how we met?"

"Okay, I'll give you that one, but you're just being pedantic. That's not how you met."

"I know, I'm sorry." She takes a sip of her tea. "But

I think it's going well. He messaged me just to say goodnight and everything."

A small blush rises to my cheeks. "Evander did the same."

"He did?" Delighted surprise comes through her question.

I pick up my phone and pull up the messages, smiling to myself as I catch sight of the final one Evander sent to me before I went to sleep.

< Goodnight! Sleep well. >

I know it isn't much, but I've never had someone that texts me like that.

I hand my phone to Michaela. She lets out a little squeal, excited by the prospect.

"Oh, you have a new message," she says. "Something about your coat?" She gives me back my phone.

I frown and look down at the screen.

< I forgot to say, I have your coat. You left it at the pub last night. Do you want me to drop it around on my way into class? >

"How could I have forgotten my coat?" I ask out loud.

Michaela shrugs. "You were probably too busy wondering whether he was going to kiss you. Did he?"

"No."

"Disappointing."

"Maybe he was just waiting for the right moment?" I suggest.

"Probably. If he's messaging you already, then that's a good sign. Has he asked you out on another date yet?"

"No."

"Hmm. Maybe you should ask him this time," Michaela suggests.

"I'll think about it. But he wants to know if he should drop my coat around here now. But he can't do that. He'll see my glasses." I reach up to touch them.

"Do you really think that's a problem? He doesn't like you because you're not wearing glasses. He won't care."

"But if he has any knowledge of supernatural creatures, he'll work out what I am."

"Not everyone who wears glasses is a gorgon." She gestures to the pair she's wearing herself.

I frown. "I suppose. But I don't want to risk it. Not when I don't have more potion to drink."

"I can ask Owen if he'll help me make more," Michaela promises.

"I'm sorry, I didn't mean to assume..."

"I know," she cuts me off. "And you didn't. It's me offering, not you asking."

"Thank you, I really appreciate it."

"I'm just glad to see you having fun with someone."

I smile, reassured that my friend knows me well. "I'll tell him to hold onto it and bring it to our next date." I type out the message, shaking slightly from a combination of excitement and nerves. "Okay, done." I hit send and the message heads over in his direction.

"Is it weird to say I'm proud of you?"

I chuckle. "No, I'm proud of me too."

My phone buzzes and I glance down at it.

< Great, I can't wait! Are you free tomorrow? >

< I think so, I'll just have to check. >

< Let me know and then we can decide where to go. >

< Will do. >

I beam widely, drawing a small laugh from Michaela.

"I see you're going to be on cloud nine for the rest of the day."

"I'm sorry, I'll try and rein it in. He's asking if I'm free Friday night. Is that too soon for the potion?"

"Leave it with me," Michaela says. "But don't confirm with him until I've had a chance to talk to Owen."

"I won't," I promise. I know I'll have to tell Evander I'm a gorgon at some point, but for now, I want to see how things go. If it's never going to get serious anyway, then revealing the information puts me in a vulnerable situation that I don't need to be in.

If we go on a third date, or fourth if we're counting the original blind one, then it'll probably be time to tell him. There's a chance he'll run away screaming, but it's probably good to know whether that's going to happen before we're in too deep.

"We need to go," Michaela says suddenly, hopping to her feet. "Economics starts in fifteen minutes and we still need to get across campus."

I groan. "I don't even like Economics."

"You still have to go. Come on." She gestures to the door as she shrugs her coat on.

I pull my spare one from my wardrobe, glad I have two. I slip it on and grab my bag, ready to go with my Pixie Cups tea in my hand. I'm not sure who thought of setting up a coffee shop by the academy, but they were a genius. Everyone goes there, especially if they want a magical pick-me-up along with their drink.

We hurry out of my room and towards our lecture. I know my mind should be on my upcoming class, but I can't help my thoughts turning to a potential second date with Evander and how much fun that's likely to be.

Hopefully, I won't be too distracted and will still manage to learn something. Though maybe that's just wishful thinking.

SEVEN

THALIA

I PACE BACK AND FORTH, trying not to be too impatient with Michaela and the fact she isn't here yet. I'm supposed to be meeting Evander in twenty minutes, and I haven't managed to take the potion yet. I have to admit to being more than a little worried about it, especially as I'm not ready for the gorgon conversation.

A knock sounds and I hurry over to the door, pulling it open.

Relief floods through me at the sight of my best friend on the other side, holding a small bottle full of purple potion. It glows softly, illuminating her hand.

"I'm sorry, I'm sorry. There was a mishap involving some spillage and a wrong ingredient," she says, stepping into my room.

"It's okay, I've got twenty minutes, and the potion worked instantly last time." Which is the only thing that's keeping my panic at bay. "Are you all right? Mishaps sound dangerous?"

"Nothing to worry about. The only victim was some coriander." She holds out the potion to me.

"Thanks." I take it from her and go to unstopper it, only for it to slip through my fingers.

I watch in horror as the open bottle starts to fall to the floor.

Michaela whips out her wand and shoots a spell in the direction of the potion, but it's already too late. The only thing she manages to save is the carpet. I can't imagine the potion would have reacted well to that.

"Thalia, I'm so sorry," she says.

I shake my head. "It's not your fault." Tears spring to my eyes and I sit back on my bed, covering my face with my hands. I'm careful not to disrupt my glasses even in my despair. With Michaela here, there's no room for a mishap. The last thing I want is to turn my best friend into stone. I don't think she'll abandon me if I do, but it's still not a nice experience.

Michaela properly steps inside and shuts the door, hurrying over to sit next to me. "I'm still sorry. I know what that meant to you."

I sigh and sit back. "I can't go," I whisper.

"I can call Owen and see if he's got any left in the cauldron?" she suggests.

"A voice call?"

She chuckles. "Yes. A real voice call. On purpose."

I let out a small laugh despite the seriousness of the situation, amused by the thought of her doing that. "You don't have to. I'll just message Evander and tell him I have to reschedule. I'm sorry for wasting your time with the brewing."

"You didn't waste my time," she assures me. "I had fun with Owen, that's good as far as I'm concerned."

I'm glad she's still gotten something out of it.

I pull out my phone and start typing out the message, deleting it several times in an attempt to get it right.

Michaela reaches out and puts her hand in front of the screen. "There is another option," she says.

"What? Do you know of another spell that might help?" I ask, hope rising within me.

"No, I'm sorry I don't."

"Oh."

"What I meant was that you could go on the date anyway and just wear your glasses. You don't even have to tell him you're a gorgon, you can just say something went wrong with your contact lenses or something."

"What if he works it out anyway?" I ask, uncertainty making my voice shake.

"Then you'll have your answer about whether it matters that you are one. If he's the person you think he is, then he's not going to care. And if he's not, then it's better you know now rather than later, right?"

"You've become very wise."

"It's the lack of potions ability," she jokes. "It means that I've had to practise being wise instead. I plan on making a career out of it when everything else fails me."

I shake my head in bemusement. "You realise there are plenty of careers that don't need potion-making skills, right?"

"I do. But how many of them are going to take a witch without them?"

"Didn't they pass the discrimination law a while back that means you don't have to disclose you're a witch unless it's pertinent to the job you're applying for."

"Hmm, true. But how well does that work in practice?"

"Not being in the job market, I have no idea," I

point out. "Maybe it's something you can ask one of the career advisers about? I'm sure they're used to that kind of thing."

She nods. "True. But that's a problem for another day. You're avoiding the real issue here."

I sigh. "I hoped you wouldn't notice."

"Mmhmm, I guessed. But you're out of luck. I did, and now I'm going to convince you that you should go despite what you're worrying about."

"I just don't want to get my heart broken," I admit.

"No one wants that. But if we all avoided the things that might hurt us, we'd end up spending a lot of time miserable. Unless this is your way of telling me that you don't really want to go on a date with Evander?"

"I do," I say quickly. "I really do. We had a good time the other night, and on our blind date. I just don't want to mess it up."

"Then you definitely need to go. How can you imagine how it will feel for him if he finds out you cancelled your date because you didn't think you could trust him with the truth?"

I frown. "I've never thought about it like that." But now she's pointed it out, I can see why it's a problem.

"Of course not, you've been wrapped up in your

side of it and ignoring his. If you think you're going to have a good time on this date, then you should go. If you think there's no future with a potential relationship, then you should cancel and tell him that it's over," Michaela says.

"Thank you." I get to my feet and smooth out my dress. "How do I look?"

"Perfect. I love the way the green compliments your hair."

A small smile spreads over my face. Green has always suited me, I think it's because of pale skin and dark red hair.

"I take it this means you're going?"

I nod. "You're right. I'm going to have fun. I don't think he'll react badly to the gorgon thing, and if he does, then it's his loss and not mine." I only half believe that, but right now, that's enough.

"Good. You should get going or you're going to be late. I'll clean up the potion."

"Thanks, Mickie."

"Anything in service of your love life," she quips.

"I'll return the favour."

"I know you will." The reassuring smile on her face convinces me that she really believes that.

We say our goodbyes and I head out of my flat. Nerves and excitement war for dominance inside me, but that's not going to be the case for long. I fire off a quick message to Evander so he knows I'm not standing him up and hurry to where we're meeting.

EIGHT

EVANDER

THERE'S a brief moment of panic that Thalia isn't going to show up, which isn't helped by the fact she's a little late to meet me. But all of those thoughts disappear when she turns the corner.

I wave at her from my spot by the fountain.

As she approaches, I realise my suspicions about her wearing glasses were correct, and as I guessed, she looks adorable in them. They suit her well.

"Hey," she says.

"Hi," I respond.

"I'm sorry I'm late, I was having a potion snafu," she admits, her voice shaking a little bit. I want to reach out and comfort her, but I'm not sure we're in the right place yet.

"Do I get more details of that?" I ask instead.

She sucks in a deep breath. "Yes, but first I need to tell you something."

"That sounds ominous. Do you want to do it here, or while we make our way to the pizzeria?" I suggest, my stomach rumbling with the need to be fed.

"Here is good," she says. "So, you know the other day when we were talking about what we were and how we were going to save the conversation?"

"I do." Where is she going with this?

"Well, I need us to have the conversation."

"Right." I hope she's not going to run away when she finds out what I am.

"I'm a gorgon."

Silence fills the air as the last thing I expect to hear comes out of her mouth.

She's a gorgon.

Like me.

"That's why I was trying to take a potion. My best friend has been working with a warlock to brew me a potion that means I can look at people without my glasses on and there's no risk of them turning into stone. She just brought it to me and it spilt before I could drink it, so here I am." Her words are coming so fast that they're almost tripping over one another in an attempt to get out.

I don't blame her, it's a nerve wracking thing to tell someone.

I give her a reassuring smile. "You're a gorgon?" I ask.

"Yes, and I know that's a shock, and it's not exactly great, but..."

"Thalia," I say firmly, gaining her attention. "I'm a gorgon too." It's a relief to say it out loud and know that it isn't going to change anything.

Her mouth falls open. "What?"

I reach into my pocket and pull out a pair of glasses, holding them out so she can see the brand. There are only a few that cater to gorgon needs, which makes me certain that she'll recognise it.

"You're a gorgon?" she checks, but I can tell she believes me, she's just trying to process it.

Which is fair. The circumstances in which we met are unusual for our kind.

I nod in confirmation. "I was worried about telling you too. Though I knew you'd be fine with it. Maybe not *this* fine."

A small laugh escapes her. "It does make things a little simpler."

"I do like the idea of not being able to

accidentally turn you into stone," I agree. "I've been worrying about that."

"Me too. But you weren't wearing glasses on our dates either."

"Ah, yes. Well, I've also been having some help with that. One of my flatmates is a warlock and he's been brewing me a potion too. It's probably the same recipe." One that I didn't know existed until Owen told me as much.

"Is it a little ironic that we've both been drinking a potion we don't actually need?"

"That is a little amusing." I smile at her, more relieved than I can put into words. "I'm glad it's all out in the open."

"Me too. I'm sorry I didn't tell you straight away. It's not that I didn't trust you, or that I thought you yourself would react badly..."

"It's just that some people can be funny about it and you had no idea how I was going to react," I finish for her. "It's the same reason I didn't tell you straight away."

"I almost didn't come tonight," she admits. "When the potion spilt, I was scared. But Michaela talked me into coming anyway. She reminded me of what I knew already and that you wouldn't care what I was."

"I only care that you're yourself," I say softly as I

step towards her. "I guess we can go for pizza now. Or..."

"Or?" she prompts when I don't finish his statement.

"I was wondering how you'd feel if I kissed you?" My voice is lower than normal, affected by how close she's standing, and how much I want to make the next move.

"Isn't that supposed to be for the end of our date?" From the way she says it, I already know she isn't going to make me wait that long.

"If we both want it, why wait?"

"Kissing now won't get you out of pizza," she warns me. "Never get between a girl and cheese topped bread."

"I wouldn't dream of it," I promise.

"Good." She closes the distance between us and circles her arms around my neck, bringing her tantalisingly near.

I rest a hand on her lower back and give myself over to the instincts driving the moment. I lean in and press my lips against hers. I give myself over to the way it feels to kiss her, enjoying the closeness it brings, along with the knowledge that we're completely safe. I may be covered by the potion right now, but in the future, I won't have to worry about my glasses being knocked off while we kiss.

I don't have to worry that I'll accidentally turn her into stone. With Thalia, I'm going to be able to be completely me. Something I've wanted from a relationship for as long as I can remember.

We break apart and she pulls back but doesn't break the contact between us. She smiles widely, seeming just as content as I am.

"So I guess that's a yes to a third date?" I tease.

"We haven't even been on our second yet."

"I just thought I'd get that out there early." I can't stop the grin from taking over my face.

"I'll go on a third, fourth, and fifth date with you," she promises.

"Then I'll have to make sure each of them is good enough to get a sixth date."

"Doesn't that just stray into relationship territory anyway?" She watches me carefully for my response.

I shrug. "I've never been clear on that. If I'm not seeing anyone else, and you're not, then does it mean we're in one anyway?"

"I honestly can't tell you. I suppose it's for us to decide."

"Hmm, interesting."

"How about we go for pizza and we can discuss the ins and outs of it over that," she says. "And we both have to have garlic bread."

"I like the way you think." I pull back. "I forgot to

give you your coat." I grab it from where it's sitting on the bench next to us and hold it out for her.

"Thanks." She slips her arms into it and wraps herself up, seeming relieved to be out of the cold. I should have thought about giving her the coat first, but I got understandably distracted.

I hold out my arm and wait for her to slip hers through. It feels right to walk with her like this. And to know that we have a potential future to explore together. It's certainly not the end I expected to a blind date situation, but I couldn't be happier with how it turned out.

EPILOGUE

THALIA

THE PROSPECT of a double date with Michaela and Owen is both fun to think about, and nerve-wracking. I know Michaela likes Evander from what I've said about him, and the same is true of me for Owen from what she's said, but this is the first time we're all properly going to meet and I want it to go well.

Evander squeezes my hand. "It'll be fine," he promises.

I glance at him, reassured by his presence. The glasses change his face and make him look more youthful than without them. I like it. They're a part of him in a similar way to how my glasses are a part of me. It's not something I fully realised until I spent some time not wearing them.

My attention turns to my own glasses, as if thinking about them has made them slide down my nose. I push them back up, glad to have them on while I'm out in public.

"You know you have nothing to worry about, right?" he says.

"I know. If Michaela doesn't like you, then you're the one who needs to worry."

He chuckles. "Then I'll be on my best behaviour and not ask any strange questions," he promises.

"I like your questions."

"I know you do."

"You're thinking about one right now, aren't you?" I ask, recognising the mischievous expression on his face. "What is it?"

"If you had to choose between having snakes for hair, or turning someone into stone, which would you choose and why?"

"That's very gorgon specific," I point out.

"Now we both know the other is a gorgon, we can ask it."

"Are they friendly snakes?" I ask.

"Does it matter?" Confusion mars his features as he tries to work out why I'm asking.

"Of course it does. If they're going to bite me in the middle of the night and leave me riddled with fang marks, then they're bad snakes. If they're just going to hiss at people who make me uncomfortable, then they're good ones. I'll accept the friendly snakes, but I'll take the stone thing over the mean snakes."

He lets out a loud laugh. "All right, fair enough."

We arrive at the pub doors and he pushes it open for me to step through.

I place a hand on his chest as I go past. It's a casual touch, but one that's all the more enjoyable because of it. I've never been in this kind of situation before, and every new thing I'm discovering just makes me more certain that this is right for me.

Michaela spots us from across the room and waves us over.

"Why don't you go say hello, and I'll get us some drinks?" Evander offers.

"Thanks. Can I have a white wine spritzer?"

"Of course." He leans in and kisses my cheek. "I'll be over in a minute."

I head towards the table where Michaela sits with the dark-haired warlock she's been dating.

"Thalia, this is Owen," she says. "Owen, this is my best friend, Thalia."

"It's nice to meet you," I say. "Thank you for all your potion making on my behalf."

"Ah, so you're the friend Mickie was trying to help?" he says.

I nod.

"I'm glad I get to meet you."

I slide into one of the seats opposite the two of them.

"Here you go," Evander says, putting a glass in front of me along with his own bottle of lager. "Hi, I'm..." He trails off and starts laughing.

After a moment, Owen does the same, leaving Michaela and I sharing a confused look.

"I'm sorry," Evander says after a moment. "Owen and I are flatmates. I never realised it was him we were coming to meet."

Ah. I see.

"You're flatmates?" Michaela says.

"And friends, yes," Owen says. "Evander is who I've been making the potion for."

Understanding dawns on my friend's face, and I completely understand it. What are the chances of something like this happening?

"Wait, you never talked about who you were making the potion for?" Evander asks the two of them.

"Of course not," Michaela says instantly. "The

potion was for a gorgon, which meant that if I told Owen Thalia's name, he'd know what you were. I didn't think that was fair. And I assume he did the same out of respect for you. I certainly never asked for the same reason."

"And he didn't work it out when you came to chaperone our date?" I can't believe we've somehow managed to miss the fact that Evander and Owen know one another.

"I guess I never said Evander's name," Michaela says. "I'm not sure, it's just one of those funny coincidences."

"It's certainly that," Evander agrees. "But I'm glad it's all out in the open now."

"It's going to make hanging out together easier," Michaela says. "That's a definite advantage of our oversight."

A smile spreads over my face. She isn't wrong about that. I'll be able to spend time with my best friend, and my boyfriend at the same time without anyone feeling like the odd one out.

This isn't how I thought my time at Obscure Academy would go, but I'm not going to let such a chance at perfection slip through my fingers. I'm a gorgon who no longer has to worry about turning the people I care about into stone. Michaela's friendship has been the key to me working that out, and it only makes me love her more for it. Without her, I wouldn't have met Evander, and I certainly wouldn't feel as comfortable in my own skin.

I owe her everything, and one day, I hope to be able to pay her back.

Thank you for reading *Blind Dates For Lonely Gorgons,* I hope you enjoyed it! If you want to know about Michaela and Owen's exploits with potion making, you can in *Potion Making For Disastrous Witches,* part of the *Obscure Academy* series: http://books2read.com/potionmakingfordisastrouswitches You can also get two bonus POVs (chapters 5 & 8) from Thalia's point of view for free here: https://books.authorlauragreenwood.co.uk/ezqpzx4rli

Thank you for reading *Blind Dates For Lonely Gorgons*, I hope you enjoyed this sweet paranormal romance Valentine's Day inspired tale.

While *Blind Dates For Lonely Gorgons* is part of the *Obscure World: Holidays* series of quick paranormal holiday romance reads, it also intertwines with the events in the *Obscure Academy* series, particularly with Michaela's book, *Potion Making For Disastrous Witches*, which will explore her growing relationship with Owen, and will include Thalia as a side character! All of the books in both series can be read as standalones.

The decision to make it so that Thalia and Evander didn't have snakes for hair came mostly from the practicality of it being very obvious that they were gorgons if they did, but that was supported when I did some research and discovered that in some versions of the legends, only Medusa has snakes for hair and the other gorgons do not. They're a rarer type of supernatural than some of the others in *The Obscure World*, though I thought the existence of harpies (also from Greek legends) in the *Supernatural Retrieval Agency* series would mean that gorgons would also exist!

I do plan for there to be more *Obscure World: Holidays*, but I'm taking the approach of writing them in conjunction with the actual holidays they represent. If you want to stay up to date on when they release, you can either join Facebook Reader Group or mailing list.

And finally, I wanted to touch on the glasses issue. I spent a long time thinking about how I wanted gorgons to work in my universe before settling on the idea that they could wear special glasses in order to stop themselves from turning people into stone. I considered having a moment where Thalia realised that she wouldn't have to wear her glasses again, but as a glasses wearer myself, that didn't quite feel right. I've tried contact lenses before and they didn't make me feel like myself, which led me to realising that was probably also true for Thalia even if she wears them for another reason than me. I wouldn't want to be rid of my glasses, they're a huge part of me and my identity. Which is how Thalia ends up finishing the book still wearing them - it felt like the most realistic and emotionally right response for her to have.

Stay safe & happy reading!

- Laura

Signed Paperback & Merchandise:

You can find signed paperbacks, hardcovers, and merchandise based on my series (including stickers, magnets, face masks, and more!) via my website: https://www.authorlauragreenwood.co.uk/p/shop.html

Series List:

* denotes a completed series

The Obscure World

A paranormal & urban fantasy world where supernaturals live out in the open alongside humans. Each series can be read on its own, but there are cameos from past characters and mentions of previous events.

Cauldron Coffee Shop - Broomstick Bakery - Obscure Academy - The Shifter Season - Stonerest Academy - Harker Academy - Ashryn Barker* - Grimalkin Academy* - City Of Blood* - Grimalkin Vampires* - Supernatural Retrieval Agency* - The Black Fan* - Sabre Woods Academy* - Scythe Grove Academy*

* * *

The Forgotten Gods World

A fantasy romance world based on Egyptian mythology.
Each series can be read on its own, but there are cameos
from past characters and mentions of previous events.

Forgotten Gods - The Queen of Gods* - Forgotten Gods:
Origins*

* * *

The Egyptian Empire

A modern fantasy world set in an alternative timeline
where the Egyptian Empire never fell.

The Apprentice Of Anubis

* * *

The Paranormal Council World

A paranormal romance & urban fantasy world where

paranormals are hidden away from the human world, and are in search of their fated mates. Each series can be read on its own, but there are cameos from past characters and mentions of previous events.

The Paranormal Council Series* - The Fae Queens* - Paranormal Criminal Investigations* - The Necromancer Council* - Return Of The Fae*

* * *

Other Series

Purple Oasis (with Arizona Tape) - Grimm Academy - Beyond The Curse* - Untold Tales* - The Dragon Duels* - Speed Dating With The Denizens Of The Underworld (shared world) - Seven Wardens* (with Skye MacKinnon) - Tales Of Clan Robbins (co-written with L.A. Boruff) - Firehouse Witches* (with Lacey Carter Andersen & L.A. Boruff) - Valentine Pride* (with Lainie Anderson) - Magic and Metaphysics Academy* (with Lainie Anderson)

* * *

Twin Souls Universe

A paranormal romance & urban fantasy world co-written
with Arizona Tape. Each series can be read on its own,
but there are cameos from past characters and mentions
of previous events.

Amethyst's Wand Shop Mysteries - Twin Souls* - The
Vampire Detective*

ABOUT LAURA GREENWOOD

Laura is a USA Today Bestselling Author of paranormal, fantasy, urban fantasy, and contemporary romance. When she's not writing, she drinks a lot of tea, tries to resist French macarons, and works towards a diploma in Egyptology. She lives in the UK, where most of her books are set. Laura specialises in quick reads, whether you're looking for a swoonworthy romance for the bath, or an action-packed adventure for your latest journey, you'll find the perfect match amongst her books!

Follow the Author

- Website: www.authorlauragreenwood.co.uk
- Mailing List: www.authorlauragreenwood.co.uk/p/mailing-list-sign-up.html
- Facebook Group: http://facebook.com/groups/theparanormalcouncil

- Facebook Page: http://facebook.com/authorlauragreenwood
- Bookbub: www.bookbub.com/authors/laura-greenwood